HAMLET

Based on the play by
William Shakespeare

Adapted by Louie Stowell

Illustrated by Christa Unzner

Reading consultant: Alison Kelly
Roehampton University

Contents

Chapter 1

The dead king

It was a bitterly cold night in Elsinore, in the kingdom of Denmark. Three men huddled together on the battlements of the King's castle. They were waiting for someone.

A young man named Horatio stood with two of the King's guards. "I think you were seeing things last night," he began.

I don't believe in gho...

"Shh!" hissed one of the guards. "It's here..."

Horatio gasped. A shadowy figure had appeared beside them.

4

"It looks exactly like the King!" cried Horatio, in terror. "The *dead* King. Why are you here?" he asked the figure. "Please, speak."

But the ghost shook its head and did not reply. As the sun began to rise, he faded away into thin air.

Cock-a-doodle-doo!

"I must tell Hamlet," said Horatio. Hamlet was his best friend, and the dead King's son.

Prince Hamlet had been utterly miserable since his father died. He kept to himself and dressed mostly in black.

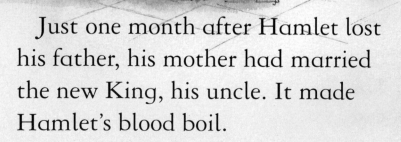

Just one month after Hamlet lost his father, his mother had married the new King, his uncle. It made Hamlet's blood boil.

How could she forget his father
so quickly? He was suspicious
about his father's death, too. It had
been so sudden. All these thoughts
churned over and over in his mind.

When Horatio came to see
Hamlet the next morning, his
friend was sitting alone and
looking very gloomy indeed.

"Hamlet," Horatio began, in a quiet voice. "I think I saw your father last night."

Hamlet leaped up. "What?"

Horatio told him about the ghost's visit the night before.

"I have to see this for myself," said Hamlet. That night, they went up to the battlements to wait.

Drunken yells echoed
around the castle courtyard.
   "What's that noise?"
asked Horatio.

Hic!

   "My uncle Claudius is having a
party to celebrate marrying my
mother," said Hamlet, bitterly.
"The guests came for my father's
funeral and stayed on."

9

As the clock struck midnight the
ghostly figure appeared once more.
   "Father?" cried Hamlet. "Speak to
me! What do you want?"
   The ghost beckoned to him and
Hamlet stepped closer, trembling.

10

"Take revenge for my murder,"
said the ghost. His voice was like
the whistling of the wind.

Hamlet's eyes widened. "Who
murdered you?"

"Your uncle," said the ghost. "My
own brother did this dreadful thing."

Chapter 2

Revenge

The ghost told Hamlet the whole story. "I was dozing in the orchard when I felt something dripping into my ear. It burned me! So I opened my eyes... and the last thing I saw was Claudius, clutching a bottle of poison."

"I couldn't even beg forgiveness for my sins," added the ghost. His voice pierced Hamlet's heart. "So now I'm being punished."

"I'll avenge you!" said Hamlet. "I swear I will."

The ghost nodded. "Kill him for me," it said, and disappeared.

Horatio came up to Hamlet.
"Well, what did he want?"
Hamlet shook his head and
his eyes darted from side to side.
"You'll tell someone," he said.

"I swear, I won't tell a soul,"
promised Horatio.
"Very well," said Hamlet, and
told him what the ghost had said.

"If you see me acting as if I'm crazy," Hamlet added, "it's just part of my plan."

"What plan?" asked Horatio.

"I'm going to pretend to be mad," said Hamlet, "so my uncle won't guess what I'm really thinking."

Horatio saw a strange look in his friend's eye. He wasn't sure if Hamlet would have to pretend.

Chapter 3

A prince in love?

"King Claudius! King Claudius!" called a voice. It was Polonius, the King's adviser. He came rushing into the throne room. "Hamlet has gone mad," he announced. "And I know why."

The King started. "Mad?"

"Yes!" panted Polonius. "He
came into my daughter Ophelia's
chamber and ranted and raved."

"He's mad with love, you see,"
explained Polonius.

"Ah." The King sounded relieved.
"I would like to see this for myself."

Polonius smiled smugly. "Let's send Ophelia to Hamlet's room, then hide and watch them. You'll soon see how the poor boy has lost his wits over my beautiful girl."

The King wasn't sure if he entirely believed Polonius, but he agreed to the plan. They hid behind a curtain to spy on Hamlet.

18

Ophelia went up to him and greeted him. Hamlet certainly started to rant and rave, but not like a man who was mad with love.

"Go away!" he screamed at her.

"You women are all the same!"
Hamlet spat. "You paint your
faces, you lie and you betray us."
     When he'd finished yelling,
he stalked away, muttering to
himself. Ophelia stared after him
in shocked silence.

The King turned to Polonius.
"He doesn't *sound* like he's in love."

Secretly, the King was worried.
Was Hamlet angry with his
mother for remarrying so quickly?
Did he suspect something about his
father's death?

He should send Hamlet away,
just in case. But that might not
be enough. Perhaps he should get
Hamlet out of the way for good...

Chapter 4

The play

Hamlet was alone in a chilly room in the castle, cursing himself. "I'm useless!" he muttered. "I promised my father I would kill Claudius. What's stopping me?"

22

A voice of doubt was whispering in his ear. What if the ghost wasn't his father, but a devil in disguise? "I need proof that the ghost was telling the truth," he thought.

An idea struck him. A troop of actors was visiting the castle. "I'll ask them to put on a play about a man who poisons a king," he thought. "If Claudius looks guilty, I'll know he did it."

Hamlet went to see the leader of
the troop and gave him a script.
"Will you put on this play?"

"Of course, my lord," said the
actor, with a bow.

That night, the King and Queen
settled down to watch the play.
Hamlet sat beside them, so he
could keep an eye on the King.

24

Music struck up and the play began. An actor playing the villain crept up to the man who was playing the king. The fake king snored loudly and the villain poured poison in his ear.

Hamlet glanced at his uncle. He had gone pale.

"How do you like the play?"
asked Hamlet with a bitter smile.

The King did not reply. He
stood, stumbled over his chair and
left the room.

"The ghost told me the truth,"
thought Hamlet. "Now I can
have my revenge." He got up and
followed Claudius.

Chapter 5

A rat!

The King hurried along the castle
corridors to the chapel. His heart
was heavy with guilt. At the
chapel, he knelt before the altar
and tried to pray.

Hamlet was not far behind. He came into the chapel and watched his uncle.

"I could do it now," he thought. "He won't hear me coming."

But Hamlet shook his head. "If I kill him while he's praying, he'll go straight to heaven. That isn't a punishment. It's a reward." And he decided to wait.

Oh God, forgive me!

When the King returned to his throne room, Polonius was waiting for him. "I've got another plan," he said, looking pleased with himself.

Claudius groaned.

"We should send Hamlet to talk to his mother," Polonius went on. "Perhaps she can get him to stop behaving like a lunatic? I'll hide and listen in."

So Hamlet was summoned to his mother's room. He strode in with a face like thunder.

"Hamlet, you've offended your step-father," his mother scolded.

"Mother, you've offended my father – by marrying my uncle," replied Hamlet. He grabbed her. His eyes flashed with fury.

"Help, help!" cried his mother.
There was a noise from behind
the curtain.

Hamlet whipped out his sword, crying, "What's that? A rat?" He plunged his sword through the curtain... and into Polonius.

There was a terrible groan.

"Was that the King?" said Hamlet and he pulled the curtain aside.

"Oh," he said, as Polonius's body fell out. "It's you." He shrugged. "I'm sorry I killed you, but it can't be helped." He began to drag the dead man out of the room.

"He's mad!" sobbed the Queen.

When the King heard what had
happened, he called for Hamlet.
"Where is Polonius's body?" he
asked. But no one knew
where Hamlet had hidden it.

"He's at dinner," said Hamlet.
He grinned. "With the worms.
Only they're eating him, not the
other way around."

The King saw his chance. "Hamlet," he said. "My dear son… You cannot possibly stay in Denmark now. I'll send you to England to keep you safe."

Hamlet agreed to go. But he was sure that the King was up to no good.

Chapter 6

The mad sister

The King and Queen were in the
throne room some days later, when
Polonius's daughter, Ophelia,
drifted in. Her hair was wild and
tangled. She looked as though
she'd been dragged through
a hedge.

She began to sing a song as she walked. Clutching bunches of wild flowers in her hands, she handed a bloom to the Queen.

Everyone watching realized that Ophelia had lost her mind.

A furious pounding on the door
broke into her song. "Laertes is
here!" called a guard.

Laertes was Ophelia's brother. He
stormed into the throne room.

"Where is my father's body?"
Laertes demanded. "I heard he was
killed. Who did it?"

Before the King could answer,
Laertes saw Ophelia.

She gazed at him, hardly even
seeing him. Laertes was horrified.

"Oh, my dear sister, what's
happened to you?" he gasped.

"Would you like a violet?" she asked. Then she shook her head. "I can't give you a violet. They all withered when my father died."

"She's mad with grief," said the King. "I'm sorry to tell you, Laertes, Hamlet killed your father. It's all his fault."

"I'll kill Hamlet for doing this!" Laertes swore.

The King waved him close and whispered, "Don't worry. He will get what he deserves soon."

The King smiled. At any moment, his men would be killing Hamlet on board the ship to England. Or so he thought...

"Prince Hamlet is here!" came a cry from the courtyard. "Prince Hamlet has returned from England."

The King's eyes widened with surprise. Laertes began to mutter under his breath about what he planned to do to Hamlet. The Queen rushed out to greet her son.

Hamlet's friend Horatio smiled. He was standing quietly near the King, holding a letter from Hamlet that explained everything.

...The King's men turned on me, as I suspected they would. But at that very moment we were attacked by pirates and I managed to stow away on the pirate ship. I am on my way home. When I return, I will take my revenge!

Yours ever,

Hamlet

The King spoke quietly to Laertes. "Hamlet might still be alive, but I have a plan to change that. You must challenge him to a duel."

"But what if I don't kill him?" said Laertes.

"I'll dip one of the blades in deadly poison," said the King. "Even if you merely graze his skin, he will die."

The King rubbed his hands. "If he wins without a scratch, I'll offer him a drink laced with poison."

Laertes thought about this for a moment. It seemed a dishonest way to get his revenge.

But his thoughts were interrupted by the Queen. She burst into the room, tears streaming down her face. "Ophelia has drowned herself!" she sobbed.

"They found her floating like a mermaid in the lake. Dead! Oh poor Ophelia!"

Laertes gripped his sword hilt. "I'm ready to challenge Hamlet," he told the King. "I will kill him, if it's the last thing I do."

49

Chapter 7

The duel

Hamlet was out walking with
Horatio. They passed through a
graveyard where two men were
hard at work, digging a grave.

One of the gravediggers threw an old skull up out of the grave.

Hamlet caught it. "Hey!" he called. "Whose skull is this?"

"A court jester who died years ago," the man replied. "His name was Yorrick."

Yorrick?

Hamlet felt sad. "Poor Yorrick. I knew him, Horatio – so full of fun when he was alive." He pointed at the skull. "Look, he's still grinning."

The sound of chanting floated across the graveyard. A funeral procession was coming closer. Hamlet recognized the King, the Queen... and Laertes.

"Oh, Ophelia," Laertes wept. Hamlet rushed over to the coffin. "That's Ophelia?" he said.

"You!" Laertes spat. "Go to the devil!" He leaped at Hamlet, pushing him into the empty grave and jumping after him.

"Hamlet, don't!" said Horatio, as guards pulled the pair out.

"You can settle this like gentlemen," the King declared. "I order you to fight a duel."

Chapter 8

The poisoned sword

That afternoon, the King, the Queen and their courtiers came to watch Hamlet and Laertes fight.

Two swords were laid out for them. Laertes knew which one to pick. "I'll take this one," he said.

The men faced each other, their shining swords held high.

"Good luck!" called the King. "And if you win, Hamlet, I have a delicious drink waiting, to toast your victory."

Hamlet and Laertes began to fight. With a quick thrust, Hamlet cut Laertes' arm with his blade.

"A hit!" everyone cried. "First blood! Well done Hamlet!"

The King was worried. He raised the poisoned cup. "Here, have a drink before you go on, Hamlet."

"No, I'll drink when the fight is over," said Hamlet.

The men circled each other. Hamlet struck again, this time on Laertes' shoulder.

Hurrah for Hamlet!

Before the King realized it was happening, the Queen had picked up the poisoned cup. "To my son!" she cried, and gulped down a mouthful of the deadly drink.

As the Queen drank, Laertes
swiped with his sword and the
blade bit into Hamlet's side. It
wasn't a deep wound, but the
poison was in Hamlet's blood.

Hamlet struck back and their
blades clashed together. The force
of the blow knocked both swords to
the ground.

When they picked them up
again, Laertes had Hamlet's sword
in his hand and Hamlet was
clutching the poisoned blade.

With a grunt, Hamlet struck
Laertes. As the sword grazed
his arm, Laertes recognized the
weapon. "I'm dying," he thought.

Then the Queen began to groan in agony. "That drink... Oh my dear Hamlet, I've been poisoned."

"There's a traitor here," cried Hamlet. "Find him!"

"There *is* a traitor," said Laertes. "And it's me. I plotted with the King to kill you. My sword was poisoned. We're both dying. I... I am so sorry."

Hamlet looked down at the poisoned blade. Suddenly, everything became clear. He had nothing to lose now, and he knew what he had to do.

"This is for my father," he called. He rushed at the King, stabbing him with the poisoned sword. The King cried out.

The King and Queen slumped in their thrones, life ebbing away. Hamlet staggered and fell and Horatio rushed to his side.

"If you are dying, I'll die with you," cried Horatio. He picked up the cup that the Queen had put down. "I'll drink this poison."

Hamlet raised a hand. "Don't, please. I want you to tell the world my story," he said. His voice was growing weak.

"Remember me," he whispered. "The rest is silence."

William Shakespeare
1564-1616

William Shakespeare was born in Stratford-upon-Avon, England, and became famous as an actor and writer when he moved to London. He wrote many poems and almost forty plays which are still performed and enjoyed today.

Internet Links

You can find out more about Shakespeare by going to the Usborne Quicklinks website at **www.usborne.com/quicklinks** and typing in the keywords 'yr shakespeare'. Please note that Usborne Publishing cannot be responsible for the content of any website other than its own.

Designed by Michelle Lawrence
Series designer: Russell Punter
Series editor: Lesley Sims

First published in 2009 by Usborne Publishing Ltd., Usborne House, 83-85 Saffron Hill, London EC1N 8RT, England. www.usborne.com
Copyright © 2009 Usborne Publishing Ltd.